The Little Lambs'
GREAT
NEW ZEALAND
EASTER
ACTIVITY BOOK

Illustrated by
ALEKSANDRA SZMIDT

Dot to Dot

Starting at the number 1, follow the numbers
and join the dots to finish the picture.

Colour Me In!

Word Scramble

Finish rearranging the letters to spell out the words.

REEATS   _ _ S _ _ R

NYBNU   _ _ N _ _

KETSAB   _ A _ K _ _

TORRAC   _ _ _ _ O T

MALB   L _ _ _

Make Your
Whānau an Easter Egg

Colour in each egg and write the name
of the person it is for in the space underneath.

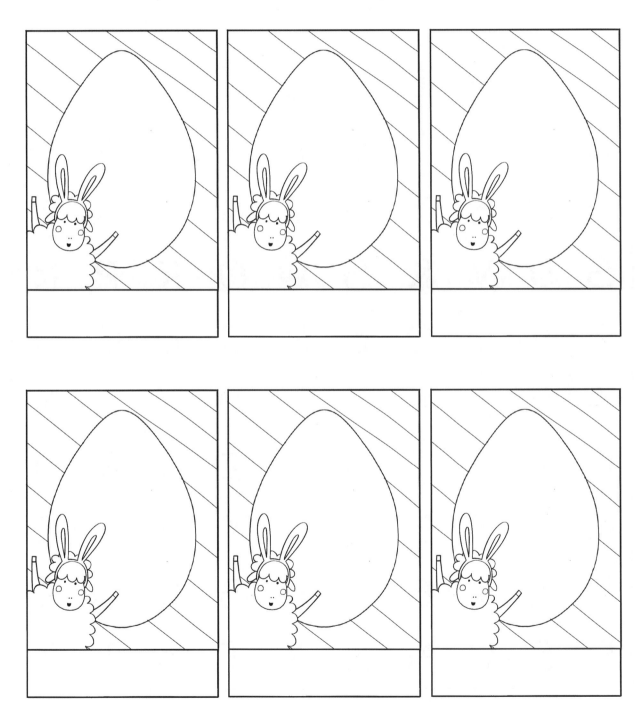

Word Search

Find these 6 words in the puzzle.

EASTER   CARROT
BUNNY   LAMB
BASKET   EGGS

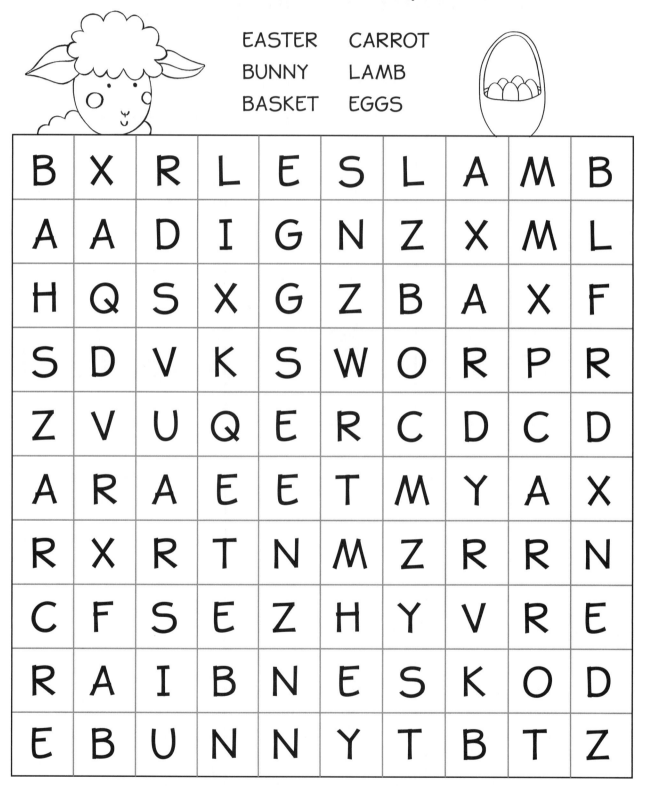

B	X	R	L	E	S	L	A	M	B
A	A	D	I	G	N	Z	X	M	L
H	Q	S	X	G	Z	B	A	X	F
S	D	V	K	S	W	O	R	P	R
Z	V	U	Q	E	R	C	D	C	D
A	R	A	E	E	T	M	Y	A	X
R	X	R	T	N	M	Z	R	R	N
C	F	S	E	Z	H	Y	V	R	E
R	A	I	B	N	E	S	K	O	D
E	B	U	N	N	Y	T	B	T	Z

Words can go horizontally, vertically, or diagonally.
Words can share letters as they cross over each other.

Colour Me In!

Which Bird Am I?

Match the bird to its name.

Kākāpō

Kererū

Kiwi

Penguin

Tūī

Fill in the Letters
to Finish the Sentence

Five little lambs went
hunting for Easter _ _ g _.

Birds have _ _ n _ _ to fly.

Rabbits are also known as b _ _ _ _ _ _.

Dot to Dot

Starting at the number 1, follow the numbers
and join the dots to finish the picture.

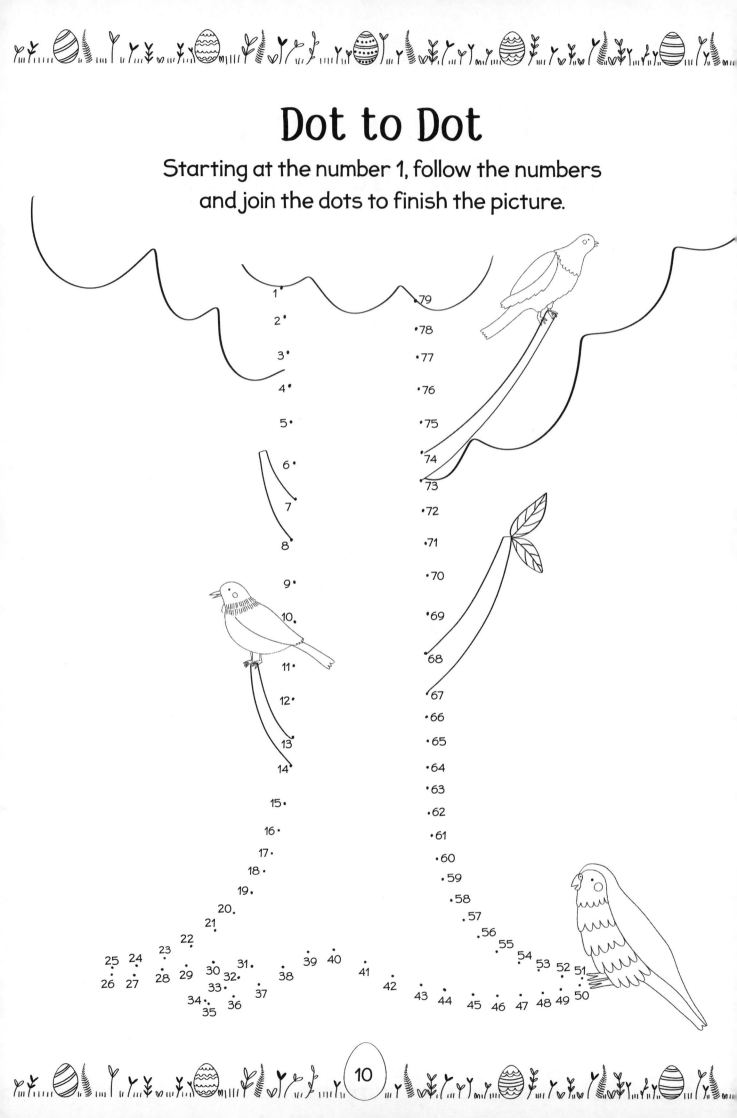

Colour Me In!

Colour In an Easter Egg
for Each Bird

Spot the Difference

Can you spot 8 differences between these 2 pictures?

Finish the Sheep

Use the grid to help you draw the other half of the sheep.

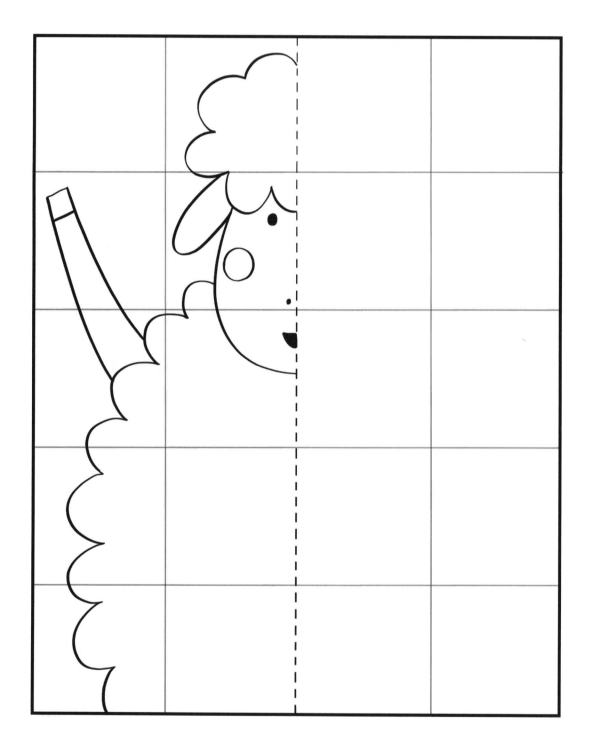

Colour Me In!

Colour by Shape

Colour in the egg using the following colour key.

RED   ORANGE   YELLOW   GREEN   BLUE   PINK

Crossword

Use the clues below to fill in the crossword grid.
Letters are shared when the words intersect.

ACROSS

2. Which animal makes the sound 'baa'?

5. Which New Zealand bird can swim?

DOWN

1. What can you collect eggs in?

3. What do you find in a nest?

4. Which New Zealand bird is flightless?

Maze

Help the lambs get to the basket.

Colour Me In!

Colour in the nest and draw your own bird.

Dot to Dot

Starting at the number 1, follow the numbers to join the dots and finish the picture. There are 3 items to finish.

Make Your Own Bunny Ears

Cut out the pieces and glue or tape the ears to the strips to create a Bunny Ears crown!

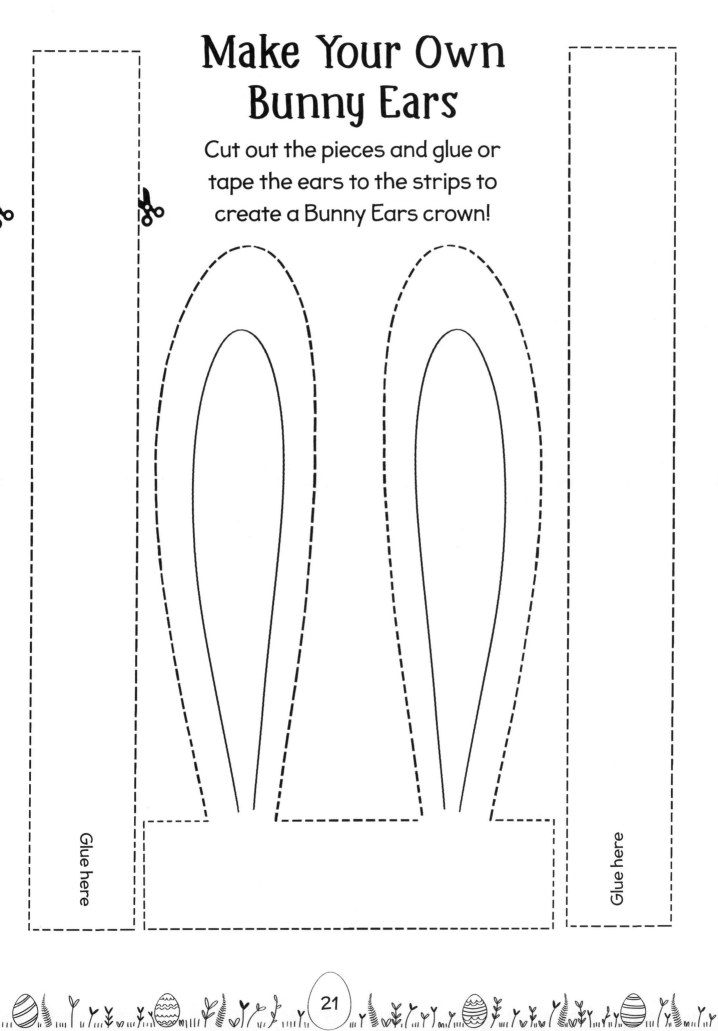

Glue here

Glue here

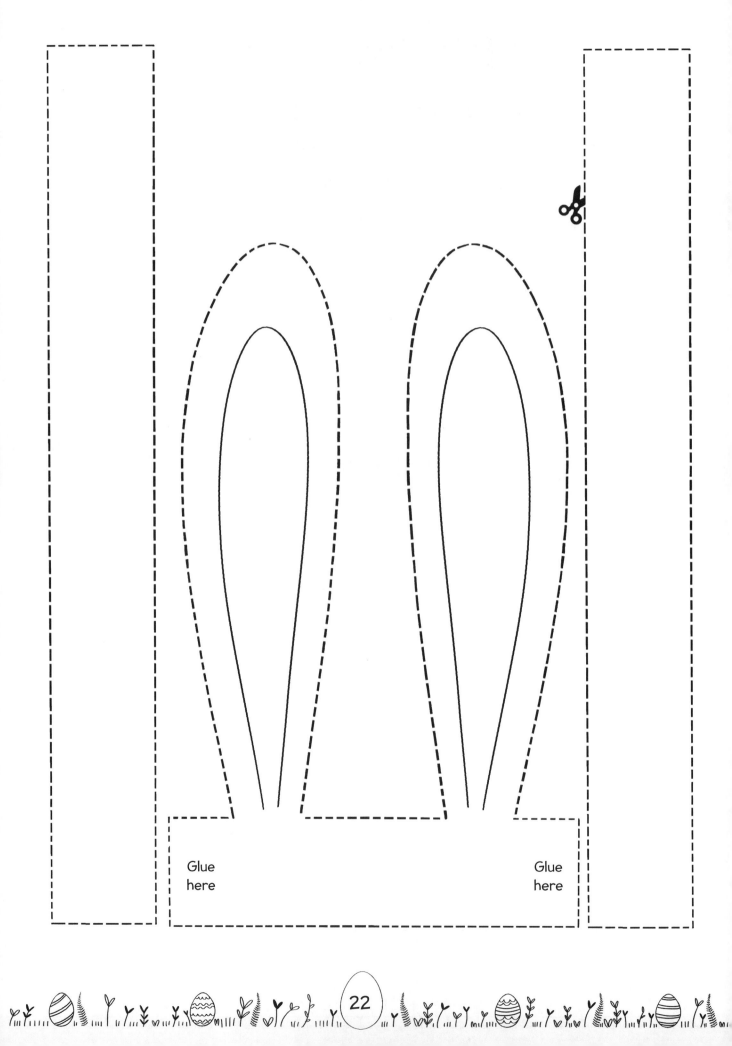

Glue
here

Glue
here

Colour Me In!

Odd One Out

Which one in the row is not the same as the others?

(1)

(2)

(3)

(4)

Find the Eggs

Can you spot the missing eggs in this picture?
There are 32 to find in total.

Colour Me In!

Word Search

Find these 5 words in the puzzle.

KĀKAPŌ   PENGUIN

KERERŪ   TŪĪ

KIWI

Q	N	X	M	B	Ō	U	W	M	K
A	I	C	I	P	F	S	F	J	V
L	N	W	Ā	E	Ī	C	Q	P	X
D	B	K	J	W	Y	L	Y	E	P
W	Ā	V	Q	X	T	Ī	O	N	S
K	E	R	E	R	Ū	L	G	G	T
Y	H	P	F	T	J	V	S	U	W
R	Ō	F	O	F	A	Z	D	I	Ā
Y	C	H	Ī	F	Ē	A	P	N	W
K	I	W	I	N	W	Q	H	E	H

Words can go horizontally, vertically, or diagonally.
Words can share letters as they cross over each other.

Spot the Differences

Can you spot 9 differences between these 2 pictures?

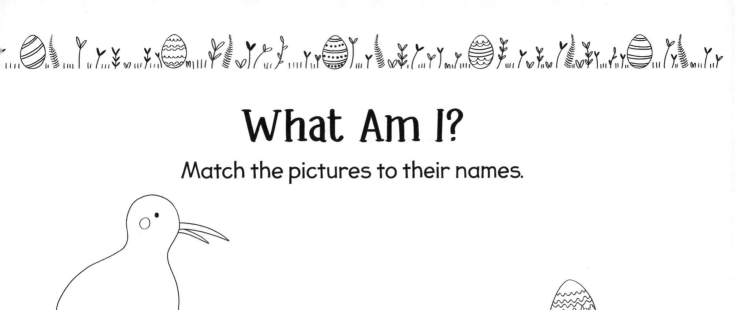

What Am I?

Match the pictures to their names.

Basket

Easter egg

Penguin

Kiwi

Nest

Tūī

Lamb

Colour Me In!

Finish the Penguin

Use the grid to help you draw the other half of the penguin.

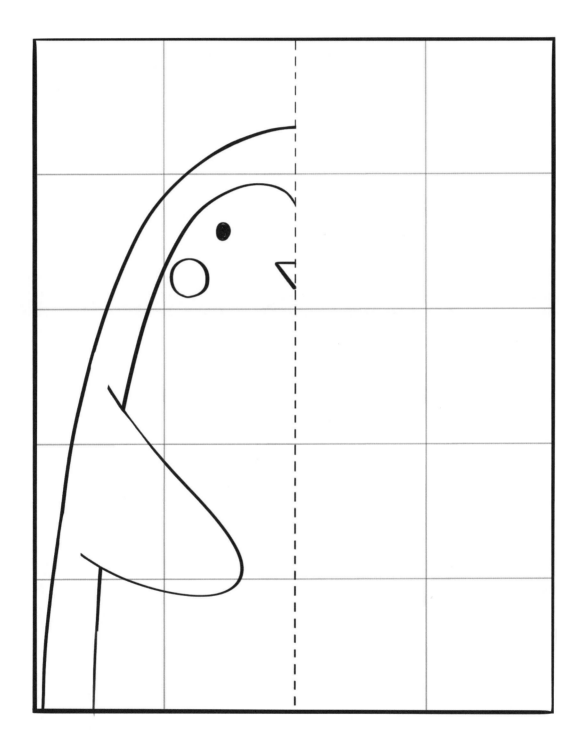

Dot to Dot

Starting at the number 1, follow the numbers
and join the dots to finish the picture.

Make Your Own Memory Game

Colour in the cards on this and the next page.
Cut out each card. Place the cards with the sheep facing up
and flip over to try and find the matching pair.

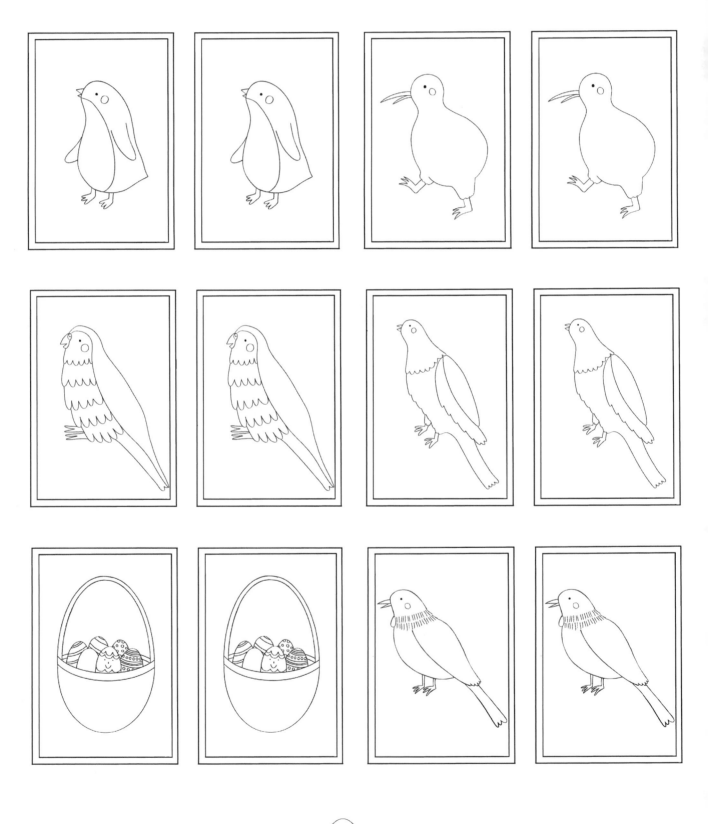

Make Your Own Sign

This room belongs to

_____

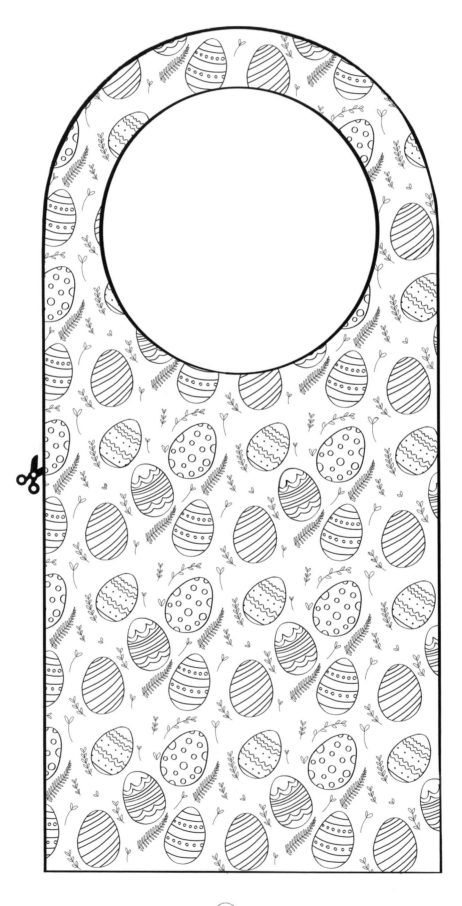

Colour Me In!

Maze

Help the Tūī get to the nest.

Make your own puzzle

Colour in the image and then cut along the gridlines
to make your own puzzle pieces.

Colour Me In!

Dot to Dot

Starting at the number 1, follow the numbers
and join the dots to finish the picture.

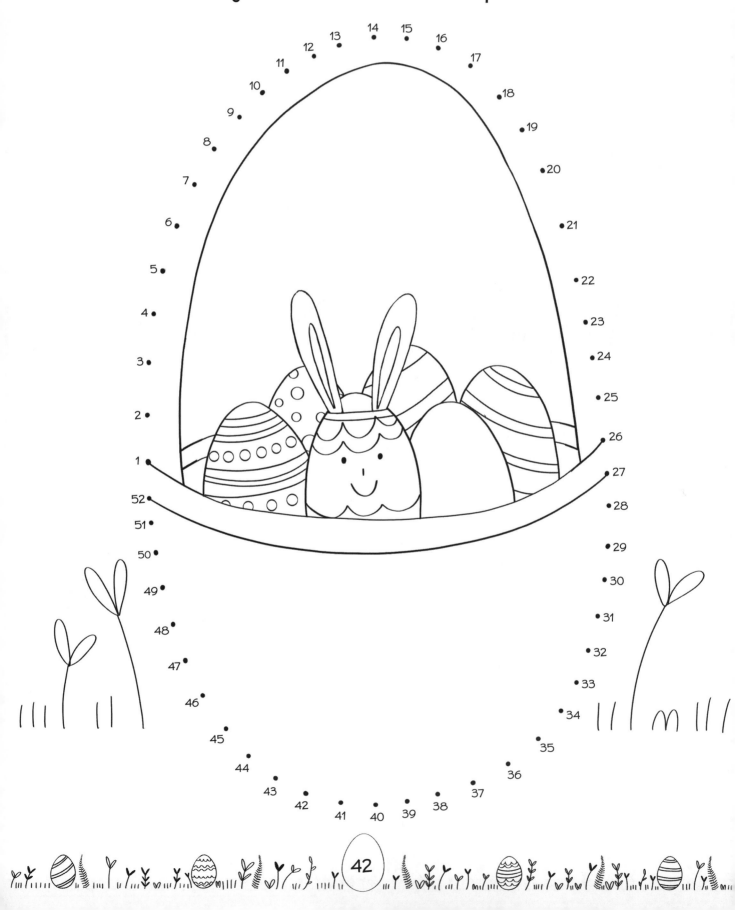

42

Easter Quiz

What do you call a group of lambs?

_____

How many Easter eggs are on this page?

_____

What sound do lambs make?

_____

Can kiwi fly?

_____

Colour Me In!

Answers

Page 4: WORD SCRAMBLE

1. Easter
2. Bunny
3. Basket
4. Carrot
5. Lamb

Page 6: WORD SEARCH

Page 8: WHICH BIRD AM I?

Starting at the top, moving clockwise:

1. Penguin
2. Kererū
3. Kākāpō
4. Tūī
5. Kiwi

Page 9: FILL IN THE LETTERS TO FINISH THE SENTENCE

1. Five little lambs went hunting for Easter EGGS.
2. Birds have WINGS to fly.
3. Rabbits are also known as BUNNIES.

Page 13: SPOT THE DIFFERENCE

Page 17: CROSSWORD

ACROSS
2. Lamb
5. Penguin

DOWN
1. Basket
3. Eggs
4. Kiwi

Page 24: ODD ONE OUT

1.   The bird
2.   The spotty egg
3.   The watering can
4.   The lamb

Page 25: FIND THE EGGS

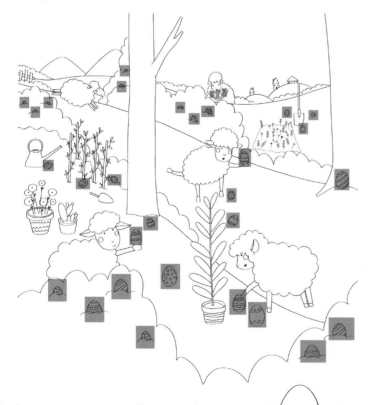

Page 26: WORD SEARCH

KĀKĀPŌ   PENGUIN
KERERŪ   TŪĪ
KIWI

Q	N	X	M	B	Ō	U	W	M	K
A	I	C	I	P	F	S	F	J	V
L	N	W	Ā	E	Ī	C	Q	P	X
D	B	K	J	W	Y	L	Y	E	P
W	Ā	V	Q	X	T	Ī	O	N	S
K	E	R	E	R	Ū	L	G	G	T
Y	H	P	F	T	J	V	S	U	W
R	Ō	F	O	F	A	Z	D	I	Ā
Y	C	H	Ī	F	Ē	A	P	N	W
K	I	W	I	N	W	Q	H	E	H

Page 28: SPOT THE DIFFERENCE

Page 29: WHAT AM I?

Starting at the top, moving left to right:

1.   Kiwi
2.   Easter egg
3.   Nest
4.   Penguin
5.   Lamb
6.   Basket
7.   Tūī

Page 43: EASTER QUIZ

1.   Flock
2.   10
3.   Baa
4.   No

A Moa Book
Published in New Zealand in 2022
by Hachette Aotearoa New Zealand
(an imprint of Hachette New Zealand Limited)
Level 2, 23 O'Connell Street, Auckland, New Zealand
www.hachette.co.nz

Illustrations copyright © Aleksandra Szmidt 2022

Based on the picture book *The Little Lambs' Great New Zealand Easter Egg Hunt*
by Yvonne Mes and Aleksandra Szmidt, copyright © 2021

A catalogue record for this book is available
from the National Library of New Zealand.

978-1-86971-484-0 (paperback)

Cover and internal design by Vida & Luke Kelly Design
Printed in China by Toppan Leefung Printing Limited